CASTLES

CASTLES
A RED FOX BOOK 978 0 099 43942 4

First published in Great Britain by Hutchinson,
an imprint of Random House Children's Books

Hutchinson edition published 2006
Red Fox edition published 2007
3 5 7 9 10 8 6 4 2

Red Fox Books are published by Random House Children's Books,
61–63 Uxbridge Road, London W5 5SA,
a division of The Random House Group Ltd,
in Australia by Random House Australia (Pty) Ltd,
20 Alfred Street, Milsons Point, Sydney, NSW 2061, Australia,
in New Zealand by Random House New Zealand Ltd,
18 Poland Road, Glenfield, Auckland 10, New Zealand,
in South Africa by Random House (Pty) Ltd, Isle of Houghton,
Corner Boundary Road & Carse O'Gowrie, Houghton 2198, South Africa,
and in India by Random House India PVT Ltd, 301 World Trade Tower,
Hotel Intercontinental Grand Complex, Barakhamba Lane,
New Delhi 110001, India

THE RANDOM HOUSE GROUP Limited Reg. No. 954009
www.kidsatrandomhouse.co.uk

A CIP catalogue record for this book is available from the British Library

Printed in Singapore

Visit Colin's website at www.colinthompson.com

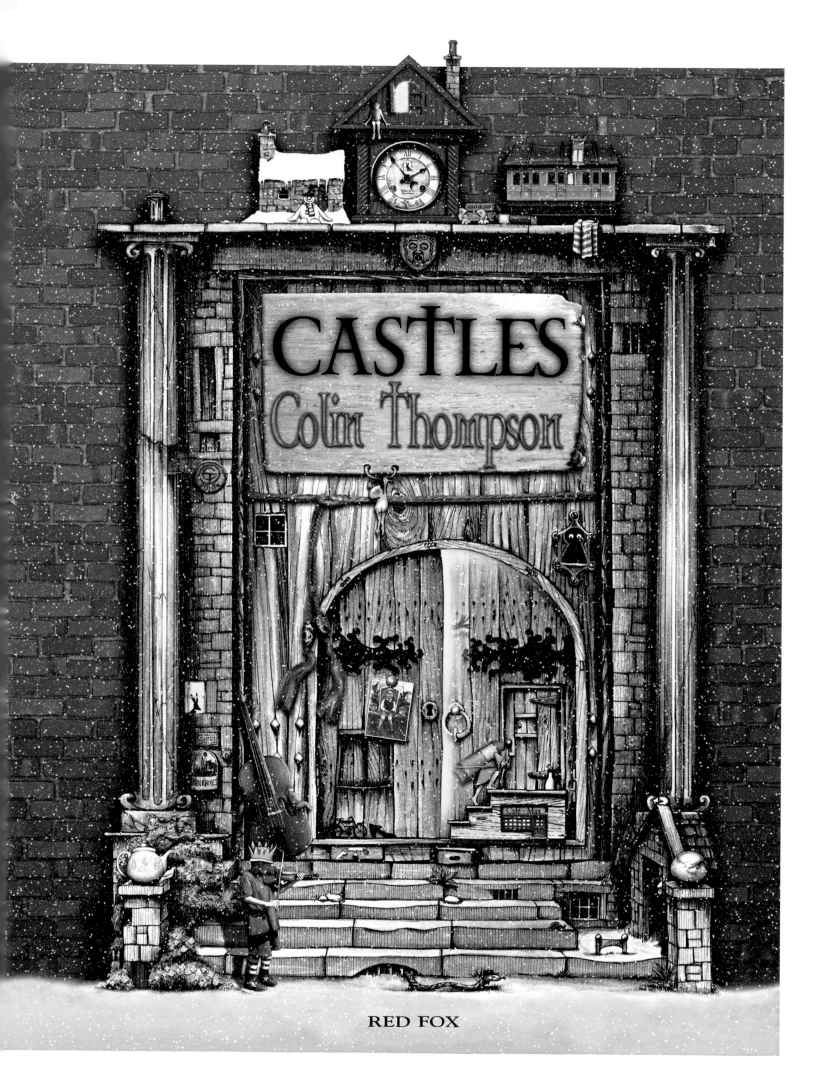

CASTLES
Colin Thompson

RED FOX

For

Holly &
Lachlan

&

Welcome
to
Max 2

Three Men in a Moat

The Mayor of Ilebridge

1

Every castle has a king, a queen, a prince and a princess.

2

Every king, queen, prince and princess is wearing a crown.

CASTLE CURES No.7
For Moats in the Eye

Café - Max

3

Of course there will only be one king and queen, but there may be more than one prince and princess — a lot more.

CASTLE CURES No.6 TURRETS SYNDROME

4

They are not all human.

MOATS open with care

DRAWBRIDGES

5

They may not even be living creatures.

6

There are more than 100 kings, queens, princes and princesses.

7

See if you can find them all.

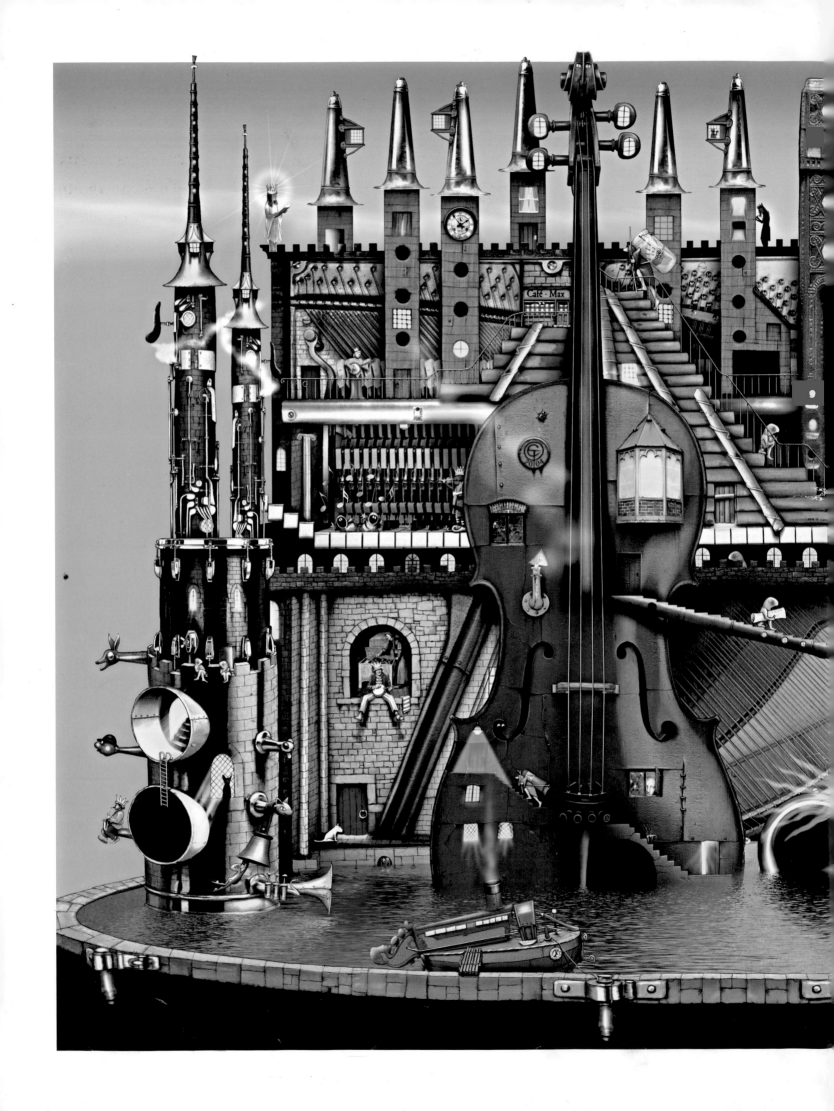

THE MUSIC CASTLE

This amazing castle stands on top of a mountain in Patagonia. It was built by a family of musicians who were tired of the neighbours complaining about their terrible music.

It is three weeks by donkey to the nearest house so now the family can play as loudly as they like without disturbing anyone. All except the colony of giant Patagonian bats that lives in a nearby cave. The bats don't mind the music as it is so bad that it encourages them to hibernate each winter.

THE MUSHROOM CASTLE

Between my house and my studio there is a path of old bricks. Sometimes very early, on damp spring mornings after a full moon, this mysterious castle appears from the cracks between the bricks.

I have no idea who lives there but by midday the entire castle and its inhabitants have vanished back into the ground.

THE CASTLE IN THE AIR

Have you ever lain on your back in the middle of summer, looking up at the empty blue sky, and felt a raindrop land on your face – but there isn't a cloud in sight?

Well, what you can feel are drops of water from the waterfalls of the Castle in the Air

as it floats by so high above you that you can't even see a dot.

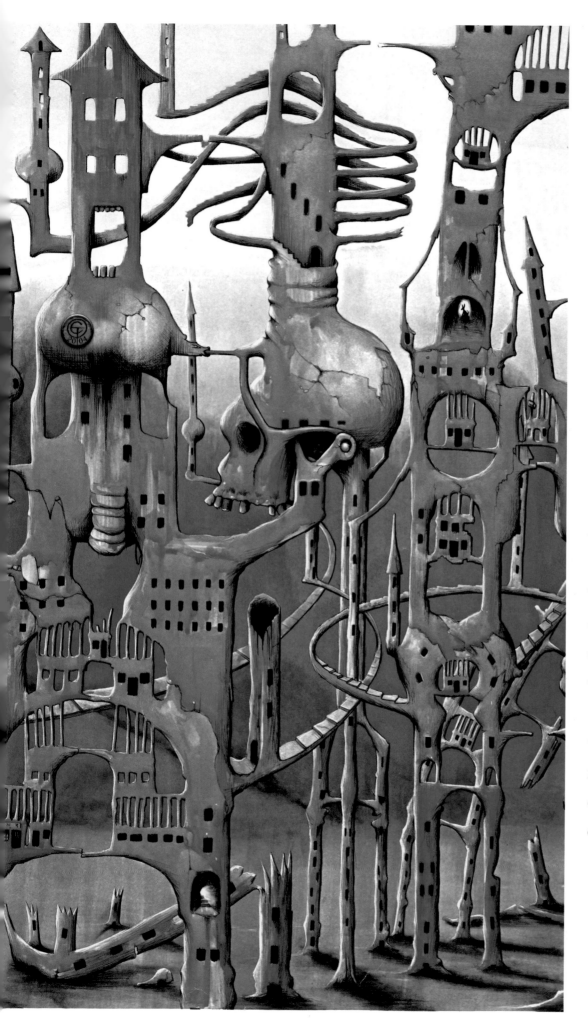

THE RED CASTLE

Most people don't believe there has ever been life on Mars. But scientists keep looking and hoping, even sending out space robots to dig around in the dust.

But they never find anything more than some tiny bacteria because they are looking in the wrong place.

Hidden away in a deep, narrow valley on the winter side of the planet are the ruins of a great city. The buildings have almost crumbled into red dust and the people have turned into fossils.

This picture shows all that remains of the fantastic Red Castle that once stood guard at the entrance to the valley.

THE ROSE CASTLE

I found this castle in my garden very early one morning. I raced inside to fetch my camera but when I got back the castle had vanished! So I went into my studio and painted this picture from memory.

Of course, it might not be *exactly* what the castle looked like because I only saw it for a few seconds, but it was definitely there. I even remember the princess waving to me.

THE CASTLE CASTLE

In 1127 the English king Nadread the Unreliable decided to build a castle that would make all other castles look pathetic. And to make sure everyone would know his was the best, he built it in the shape of giant letters that reached up into the clouds. The letters spelled,

'MY CASTLE IS THE BEST CASTLE IN CREATION'.

Through the ages, this magnificent castle has been attacked, worn away by time and had bits stolen; Nadread's bitter enemy King Sorman the Sneaky stole the whole word 'BEST', which is now run as a five-star hotel in Scotland; and my old house near Carlisle was actually built from the word 'THE'.

NORAH'S ARK

Most people don't know that Noah had a sister called Norah who also built an ark. Her ark was much bigger and better and had more animals than Noah's but because she was a girl no one took it seriously. When Noah realized his sister's ark was much better than his, he hid two giant mammoth woodworms on board, and Norah's Ark sank to the bottom of the sea.

If this hadn't happened many wonderful animals might still be with us today.

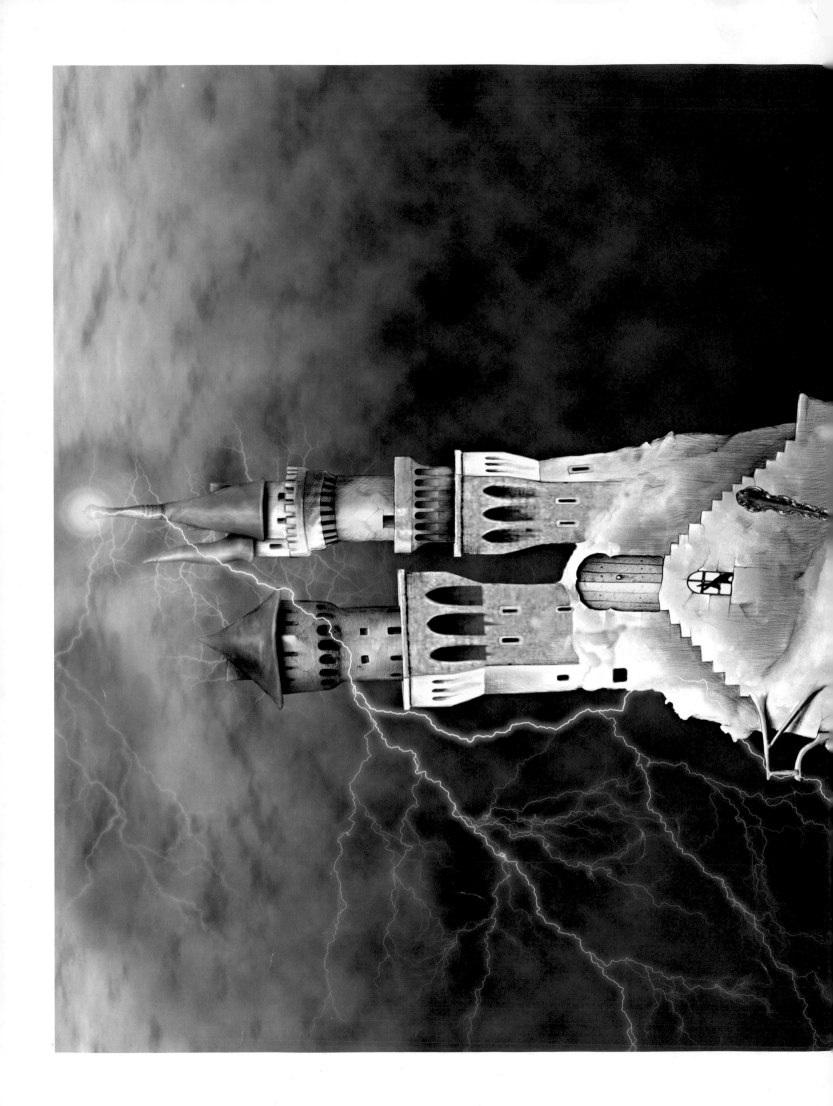

COLD POTATO MOUNTAIN

This is what can happen when sensible people tell you to stop
playing with your food and you ignore them.

THE LOST CASTLE OF ATLANTIS

The legend of Atlantis, the city lost beneath the sea, has been around for thousands of years, yet in all that time no one has found this fantastic place.

People think it is in the Mediterranean near Greece and that it was once on dry land and sank. But the reason it has not been discovered is because it is very, very small, much too small for human beings to have ever lived there.

The Castle City of Atlantis is alive and thriving in a secret rock pool in a quiet corner of Australia's Great Barrier Reef.

CASTLE COSMOS

This is the oldest castle in creation. While our ancestors were still living in caves, this castle was already many millions of years old.

Scientists believe that the builders of this castle also built planet Earth and if you look inside the glass dome you can see they made a spare, in case the original got broken. NASA has known about this for years, but has kept it secret.

Of course, life as we know it died out in the castle centuries ago. Now it is run by robot kings and queens.

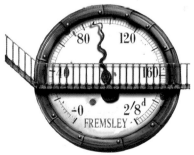

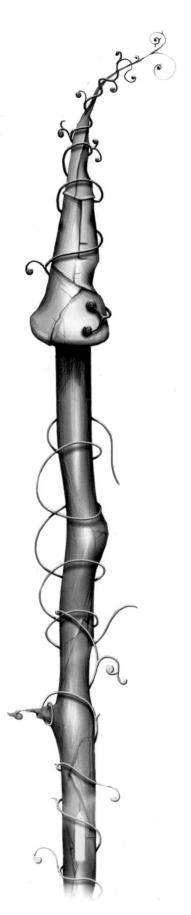